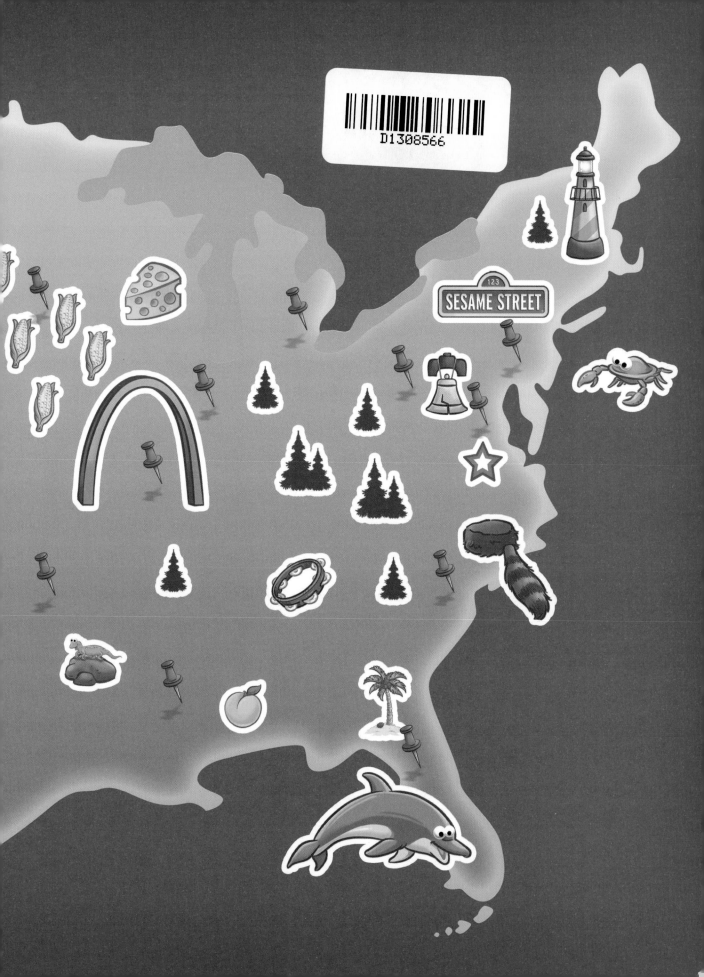

SESAME STREET

Customer Service: 1-877-277-9441 or customerservice@pikidsmedia.com

Published by Phoenix International Publications, Inc.
8501 West Higgins Road   59 Gloucester Place
Chicago, Illinois 60631   London W1U 8JJ

PI Kids and *we make books come alive* are trademarks of Phoenix International Publications, Inc., and are registered in the United States.

www.pikidsmedia.com

8 7 6 5 4 3 2 1

ISBN: 978-1-5037-5187-3

Big Bird's
ROAD TRIP

Written by Claire Winslow
Illustrated by Barry Goldberg

we make books come alive®
Phoenix International Publications, Inc.
Chicago • London • New York • Hamburg • Mexico City • Sydney

The sun is shining on Sesame Street as Big Bird has a video chat with his cousin.

"I miss you, Big Bird," says Cousin Bird. "Please come visit me in California. It's even sunnier here! And bring Radar! Walter misses his favorite cousin bear, too."

"I'd love to!" says Big Bird. "But isn't California far away from Sesame Street? Hmmm…how will we get there?"

"Did somebody say California?" asks Big Bird's friend Nina as she walks by. "I've always wanted to go there! We can take my car, Big Bird! A road trip across America will be so much fun!"

"Great idea!" says Big Bird. "I'm going home to pack!"

"Birdseed? Check," says Big Bird as he looks in his suitcase. "Roller skates? Check. Pajamas? Check! Do you have everything you need, Radar? Check? Yay! I think we're ready for our road trip!"

Big Bird and Nina's friends and family gather around the car to say goodbye.

"Elmo will miss Big Bird and Nina very much," Elmo says. Big Bird promises to video chat with his Sesame Street friends every single day, and to send lots of pictures and postcards. After a big, furry red hug from Elmo, Big Bird and Nina set off on their adventure!

Next stop: California!

Uh-oh, California is farther away than Big Bird thought!
Big Bird and Nina have only been driving for a few hours
when they need to stop to stretch their legs. It's hard to sit in a
car all day when you are eight feet and two inches tall!

Big Bird spots some kids playing soccer nearby. Soccer is a great way to stretch long legs! One of the kids comes up to Big Bird. "Hi, I'm Zahara!" she says. "Would you like to play with us?"

"Sure!" says Big Bird. "Though I'm a little bit better at basketball."

After the soccer game, Zahara invites Big Bird and Nina to meet her family.

"This is my Mama, my Baba, and my little brother Kareem," Zahara says. "And this is Asad! He thinks he's a real lion, but I know that he's just a toy."

"What do you do for fun, Zahara?" Big Bird asks.

"I like to play soccer," Zahara says. "And I love to sing!"

"I love singing too!" says Big Bird. "My favorite song is the Alphabet Song. What's yours?"

"My favorite song is in Arabic," says Zahara. "That's a language that my Mama and Baba speak." Zahara tells Big Bird that her parents grew up in a different country, and they moved to the United States before she was born.

"I've lived in the same nest my whole life," says Big Bird. "Gee, can you teach me a song in Arabic?" So Zahara does!

Soon, it's time to say goodbye to Zahara and her family. Back on the road again, Big Bird and Nina play games to pass the time.

"I spy, with my little eye, something…yellow!" says Big Bird.

"Is it you, Big Bird?" Nina asks.

Big Bird claps his wings. "You're right!" he says. "How did you guess?"

The next day, Big Bird has a video call with Elmo and his other friends on Sesame Street.

"…and then we sang a beautiful song I had never heard before!" says Big Bird. "I'll teach it to you when I get back home."

After he hangs up the phone, Big Bird
feels his tummy grumble.
"Time for lunch!" says Big Bird.
But the birdseed bag is empty!
"Don't worry, Big Bird," says Nina.
"We can stop for food at that farm stand."

At the stand, Big Bird meets Oliver. Oliver and his moms live on a farm, where they grow lots of different fruits and vegetables.

"Why don't you come over to our house for lunch?" asks Oliver's mommy.

Oliver introduces Big Bird and Radar
to his stuffed frog, Lily Pad. Then he shows
Big Bird all the animals on the farm.

"Taking care of the animals is the very best part of living on a farm," says Oliver. "My family is huge! There is Mommy, Mama, Lily Pad, one goat, two horses, nine chickens, three cats, one dog, and me!"

"Wow, my nest could never fit that many!" says Big Bird.

After lunch, Big Bird and Nina thank their new friends and wave goodbye. They get in the car and drive for a very long time. Big Bird loves to look out the window. Everything he sees looks so different from Sesame Street! Big Bird takes lots of pictures to send home.

"Big Bird, I think we might be lost," Nina says after a while. "We must have taken a wrong turn. But don't worry! We can ask someone for directions."

Nina stops the car in front of a house and asks a woman how to get to California.

"I know the way," the woman says. "I can show you on the map! Would you like some lemonade? My husband and grandchildren were just making some."

The children, Daniel and Sophie, bring out cups of lemonade and invite Big Bird to draw with them.

"I always draw animals," says Daniel, "like my seahorse, Seacookie!"

"Sometimes I draw Manny, my elephant," says his twin sister Sophie, "but I like drawing people better."

"I just love to draw!" says Big Bird. "People, animals, and monsters! Can you please pass the yellow crayon?"

Soon, it's time to say goodbye to Daniel and Sophie. It was a terrific visit, but Big Bird is excited as they drive away. They are almost to Cousin Bird's nest!

When they finally arrive, Cousin Bird and Walter
are waiting for them at the beach. Walter gives Radar
a great big bear hug.

Big Bird tells his cousin about the amazing people that he met on the way to California.

"Zahara loves to run and sing, just like my friend Zoe," says Big Bird. "Oliver's farm is like Abby's garden, but so much bigger! And my friend Elmo would have loved drawing pictures with Sophie and Daniel."

Big Bird, Radar, and Nina have a wonderful visit with Cousin Bird and Walter. Big Bird loves getting his feathers wet in the Pacific Ocean, exploring the city, and making even more new friends!

But then it's time to load up the car and, after lots of hugs, make the long trip home.

When Big Bird and Nina finally get back to
Sesame Street, everyone is there to greet them.
"I missed you all so much!" says Big Bird.
"Elmo has a surprise for Big Bird!" Elmo says,
bouncing up and down with excitement.

"Elmo made a scrapbook with all the postcards and pictures that Big Bird sent!" says Elmo. "Whenever Big Bird looks at it, he will remember his trip and all the new friends he met!"

"What a great present! Thank you, Elmo!" says Big Bird.

"The places that Big Bird went on his road trip look very different from Sesame Street," says Elmo.

"That's true," Big Bird says. "There are lots of different kinds of places all across the country, like cities, and farms, and towns, and beaches. The birdseed is different, too! And people sound different and look different. But once I got to know them, everyone I met reminded me of a friend on Sesame Street.

"You know, Elmo, the United States is really big…but kindness is the same wherever you go!"